Three Cups

Three Cups

By Tony Townsley and Mark St. Germain

Illustrated by April Willy

Tommy NELSON®

A Division of Thomas Nelson Publishers

NASHVILLE DALLAS MEXICO CITY RIO DE JANEIRO

Published in Nashville, Tennessee, by Tommy Nelson®. Tommy Nelson is a registered trademark of Thomas Nelson, Inc.

Illustrated by April Willy

Tommy Nelson, Inc., titles may be purchased in bulk for educational, business, fund-raising, or sales promotional use. For information, please e-mail SpecialMarkets@ThomasNelson.com.

Library of Congress Cataloging-in-Publication Data

Townsley, Tony.
  Three cups / by Tony Townsley and Mark St. Germain ; illustrated by April Willy.
    p. cm.
  Summary: When he is five years old, a boy's parents start giving him a weekly allowance and promise him that many adventures will follow if he puts it into three different cups. Includes author's notes on teaching children to use money responsibly.
  ISBN 978-1-4003-1749-3 (hardcover)
  [1. Money—Fiction. 2. Finance, Personal—Fiction. 3. Saving and investment—Fiction.] I. St. Germain, Mark. II. Willy, April Goodman, ill. III. Title.
  PZ7.T6674Th 2011
  [E]—dc23   2011022477

Printed in China

13 14 15 16 LEO 6 5 4

For *all* families.

On my fifth birthday,
my parents gave me a wonderful present.

They promised it would take me on many adventures.

"These three cups are from our cupboard," I said. "Is *this* my present?"

"There's more," my mother explained. "Look inside the envelope."

"We think it's time you started getting a weekly allowance," my father told me. "And every year it will grow bigger, just like you will."

"Every week we will help you divide your allowance among the three cups," Mother said. "One cup is for *savings*, one cup is for *spending*, and one cup is for *giving*."

After we discussed how to divide the money and put it in the cups, we put them in my room.

"But what about the adventures?" I asked.

"They'll come," my father promised.

Every Saturday, week after week, I got excited when it was time to put my allowance into the three cups.

Every Sunday, Monday, Tuesday, Wednesday, Thursday, and Friday . . . I forgot about the money.

One day my mother said, "It looks like your cups are filling up. Let's see how much you have."

She helped me count. I was surprised at how much was there, especially in my Savings Cup.

"I have an idea," Mother said. "Let's take a trip to the bank."

"You're rich!" said my sister.

"I think I want to keep saving my allowance in the cups," I told my mother.

"You can do that," she said. "But let's ask Mr. Duncan how the bank can help you save even more."

Mr. Duncan was the president of the bank.

He told me he could keep my money safe and
make it grow. I asked him how.

He said that when I put my money in his bank,
it would be called a "deposit." It would be placed in my
very own savings account, which would hold my money
for me just like my Savings Cup did.

Best of all, Mr. Duncan said the bank would pay me
to keep my money there! The money the bank pays is
called "interest." He explained to me how it works.

"Interest" sounded interesting to me.

After I deposited the money from my Savings Cup,
Mr. Duncan gave me a lollipop.

I asked for one for my sister, too.

"Is this the adventure?" I asked Mother.

*"It's just the beginning. Do you know how much money you
have in your Spending Cup?" she asked.*

After we got home from the bank, I counted the money in my Spending Cup. I wanted to buy a new baseball glove, but I knew I hadn't saved enough yet.

"Do you really want that glove?" Mother asked.

"I do," I told her.

Mother said if I just saved my money for a little while longer, I'd have enough to buy it.

"You could buy a doll instead," my sister said.

So I waited for one week, then two, then three. By then, I had more than enough to buy my new baseball glove.

I bought my sister a present with the money left over.

"This is an adventure," I told my mother and father.

"It's not over yet," Father said. "What about your Giving Cup?"

I was supposed to use my Giving Cup to help others.
But there were so many people who needed help,
and my Giving Cup was so small.

I went to my parents and asked them what I could do.

"A hundred things," Father said.

"A hundred times a hundred things," Mother told me.

Then I remembered that my school was collecting food
for needy families. I asked my mother if I could go with her
to the grocery store. With the money from my Giving Cup,
I bought eight cans of soup.

When I brought them to my teacher, Miss Phillips,
she asked me if I would like to help deliver all the food our
school collected.

The families we helped were happy to receive our gifts.
Helping them made me feel happy too.

That night my father asked which cup was my favorite.

"My Spending Cup," I said. "No, my Savings Cup.
But my Giving Cup made me feel good too."

*"Saving, Spending, and Giving," Father told me. "Doing all
three things as you keep growing up . . . that's the adventure."*

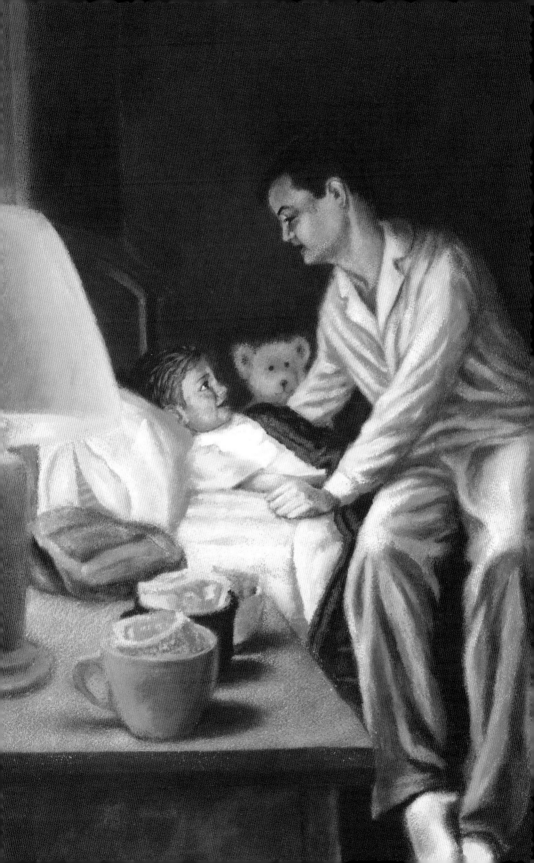

The weeks went by.

Every week I divided my allowance into my three cups.

The years went by.

Every year my allowance grew.

When I got my first job, mowing our neighbor's yard,
I also put the money I made into my three cups.

By the time I was in high school, I had bought many things
with money from my Spending Cup.

With the money from my Giving Cup, I gave to my church
and other organizations, and I helped many people.

And when I graduated from high school, I used
money from my savings account at the bank to
help pay for the college I went to.

I packed my three cups to take with me.

Today my own son turned five years old.

"Happy Birthday," I said.

"Are you ready for an adventure?"

Parent's Guide:
Getting Started with *Three Cups*

Above all else, enjoy the *Three Cups* adventure you'll share with your children. Remember, it's not how much money one has, but rather how one uses it that really matters. *Three Cups* will help establish good habits in your children, and they can continue to build on them as they grow older.

1. Pick a special day to begin: a birthday, a holiday, or another notable occasion.

2. Agree on how much your children should receive for their allowance on a weekly basis.

3. Decide (for now) how that allowance should be divided among the Savings, Spending, and Giving Cups.

4. Read *Three Cups* to your children, or ask them to read it to you. Talk about the book and answer any questions they may have. Explain that *Three Cups* is a wonderful adventure, but it is also a responsibility that you, and your children, are committing to.

5. Choose three different cups from your cupboard. Label each accordingly with the words: "Savings," "Spending," and "Giving." You might also help your children decorate their cups to make them unique and more personal.

6. Designate a safe place for the three cups; be there to help and watch your children divide their allowance money among the three cups each week, especially as you are first getting started.

7. Discuss with your children some of the things they want to save for. Encourage them to make a "wish list" of things they may use their Spending Cup money for. Talk with them about who they would like to help with their Giving Cups. Discuss tithing (giving 10 percent) to your local church, and research together other charitable organizations your children would like to help with funds from their Giving Cups.

8. Once your children have become accustomed to dividing their allowance and the cups begin to fill, agree on a good time to bring your children and their accumulated Savings Cup money to the bank.

9. During your first visit to the bank, ask a bank representative to allow your children to observe the opening of their accounts, and encourage them to ask any questions they may have.

10. As your children grow older, continue your dialogue with them about what they hope to do with their savings, spending, and charity funds. Encourage them, as their savings accounts grow, to discuss other banking options and services with your bank or other financial industry professionals.

We hope you have been touched by this book and it will encourage you to introduce your children, grandchildren, nieces, nephews, and others to the *Three Cups* program.

When you do, they are sure to have many memorable adventures that others will enjoy hearing about. We have a special section on our website reserved for these inspiring stories. Simply visit:

www.3cupsbook.com

All of us have the opportunity to make a difference in our families, communities, and in the world at large.

After reading this book, we think you'll agree: teaching children to save, spend, and give is as easy as one, two, three.